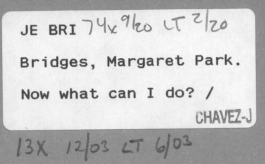

Now What Can I Do?

Now What Can I Do?

By Margaret Park Bridges

Pictures by Melissa Sweet

SeaStar Books • New York

What can I do, Mommy?
It's raining outside.

There are a million
things to do, my love.

A million? Like what?

Well, we can start
by making your bed.

Oh, Mommy—
that's not fun.

But it can be . . .
if your bed is a boat!

OK!

I'm an explorer
sailing around the world,
and my sheets are the sails . . .

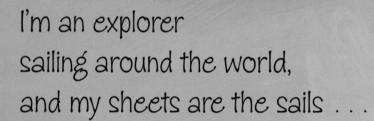

That you fold up neatly
when the wind is calm.

What else can I do, Mommy?

You can put your toys away.

What fun is that?

You're really way out west, and your toys are a herd of cattle grazing on the prairie.

And I round them all up with my giant lasso!

Yee-ha!

What else can I do, Mommy?

You can pick up the clothes
that are on your floor.

That can't be fun!

But when you're an archaeologist,
you dig deep enough to find fossils . .

And discover the oldest
dinosaur bones ever!

Or the oldest sock!

OK, what can I do now, Mommy?

You can help me fold the laundry

That doesn't sound too fun.

The fun part is shooting balls of socks into dresser drawers like real basketball players.

Look—I'm ten feet tall, doing slam dunks!

And the crowd goes wild!

SOAP

Now what can I do?

You can read a book.

Mommy, reading
is hard for me.

But when I help,
the pages turn as fast as wings.

And I can fly, bringing great stories
to kids around the world!

My superhero!

MY BOOK

What else can I do?

You can set the table.

How can that be fun?

You can spread out a blanket
on the grass by a river . . .

And have a picnic!
I'll go fishing for our dinner.

What a catch!

Then what can I do?

You can brush
your teeth.

Oh, Mommy! That's really not fun!

It is when your toothbrush is a
microphone and you're a singer.

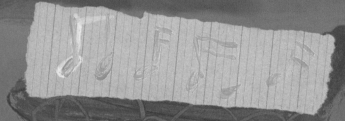

A rock star, singing
your favorite song!

I'm your
biggest fan!

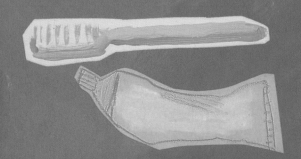

What else can I do,
Mommy?

What's so fun
about that?

It's cold way out
here on Mars!

You can put on your sleepysuit.

It's really an astronaut's
space suit that keeps you
warm and cozy.

Don't forget
to write!

OK, what else
can I do?

Now you can
snuggle into bed.

Oh, Mommy . . .

All race cars need
to rest their engines
at the end of the day.

After they've won
first place?

Yes, or they
run out of gas!

But Mommy,
why does the
day have to end?

So I can tuck in the night sky
around you like a blanket.

And the North Star
is my night-light!

Then we can always
find each other.

We did a lot of fun
things today, Mommy.

We sure did.
And you were a big help
to me, my love.

I was?

Yes—the day went by so quickly.
Now, what can we do tomorrow?

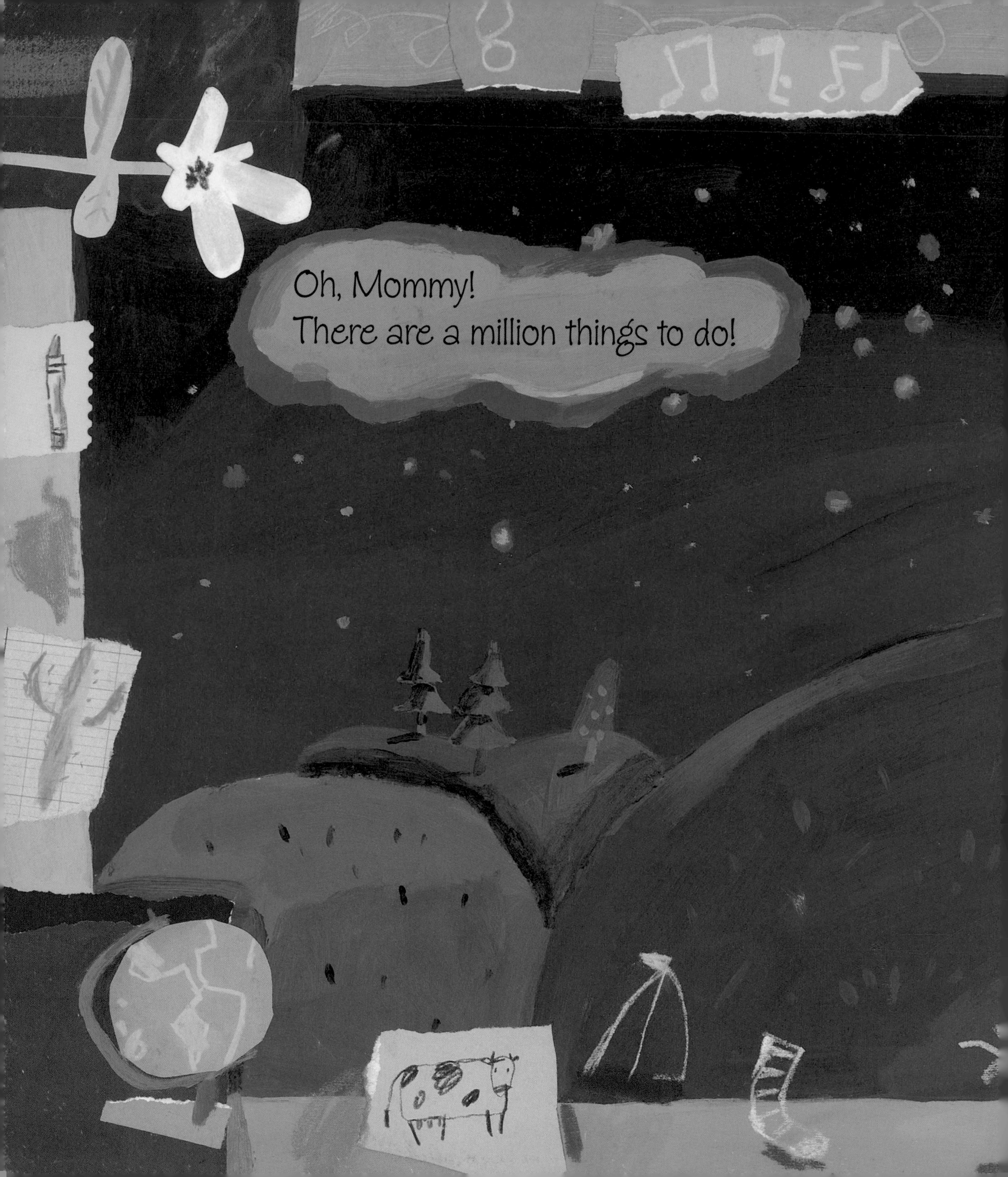

Oh, Mommy!
There are a million things to do!

For Andrea
—M. P. B.

To my friend, Ellen
—M. S.

Text copyright © 2001 by Margaret Park Bridges
Illustrations copyright © 2001 by Melissa Sweet

SEASTAR BOOKS
A division of NORTH-SOUTH BOOKS INC.

First published in the United States by SEASTAR BOOKS, a division of North-South Books Inc., New York.
Published simultaneously in Canada, Australia, and New Zealand by North-South Books,
an imprint of Nord-Süd Verlag AG, Gossau Zürich, Switzerland.

Library of Congress Cataloging-in-Publication Data is available.
The artwork for this book was prepared by using acrylics.

ISBN 1-58717-046-9 (trade binding)
1 3 5 7 9 TB 10 8 6 4 2
ISBN 1-58717-047-7 (library binding)
1 3 5 7 9 LB 10 8 6 4 2

Printed in Singapore

For more information about our books, and the authors and artists who create them,
visit our web site: www.northsouth.com